Sawbones

by

Stuart MacBride

First published in 2008 in Great Britain by
Barrington Stoke Ltd
18 Walker Street, Edinburgh, EH3 7LP

www.barringtonstoke.co.uk

ISBN: 978-1-84299-529-7

Printed in Great Britain by Bell & Bain Ltd

A Note from the Author

A couple of years ago I stayed with some friends in Iowa, eating too much barbecue and learning how to shoot the kind of guns you only get to see in movies. Ever since then I've wanted to write something dark and twisted set in the USA, and *Sawbones* is my first stab at it.

Barrington Stoke said they'd never had a serial killer book before (as it's not easy to make one work without turning the thing into a doorstop-sized lump of paper) but would I have a go? Woo-hoo! Damn right I would. This book was the result.

Most of my crime novels are set in my home town of Aberdeen. The cops are the good guys and everything has to be done by the rules. So *Sawbones* was a great excuse to throw all those rules out of the window and just have fun.

If every book was as much fun to write as this one was, I'd be a much less grumpy sod than I am.

Hope you enjoy it,

Stuart.

For Tammy, Bill and the
Original Issue Kid.

With many thanks to Rick, Mike and Pat.

Contents

Chapter 1

Soon as I see the police cruiser in the rear-view mirror I know we're fucked. Friday morning, fifteen miles out from Bloomington, Illinois and pouring with rain. Bouncing back up off the grey tarmac in the early dawn light. The cruiser holds back – must be running a check on our out-of-town number plate. I *knew* it was a bad idea to steal something with an 'I ♥ New York' bumper sticker ...

Henry's sitting beside me in the passenger seat. He hears me swearing and turns to stare out the back window. The cruiser's lights swirl red and white through the rain. The cop wants us to pull over. "God-damn it, Mark," Henry says to me. "What did I tell you?"

"Hey, don't look at me, I been driving like an old lady all the way from New Jersey. No speeding, no nothing."

"Son-of-a-bitch."

For Henry, that's pretty mild.

He runs a hand through his long, grey hair and scowls at Jack in the back seat.

"Listen up," he says, "You don't do shit unless I tell you. Understand?"

Jack isn't listening. He's checking his Glock nine mm, making sure it's loaded and ready to blow some poor bastard's head off.

Henry glowers at him. "I said, do – you – understand?"

Jack shrugs, then winces. He looks like shit with his nose all broken and two black eyes, but he's a fucking super-model compared to Brian, the guy he's sitting next to.

Henry reaches a hand back between the seats as I pull over onto the hard shoulder. "Give me the gun."

Jack doesn't look at him. "Fuck you." He doesn't sound nowhere near as cocky as he did when we started this thousand-mile-long road trip. But he's still trying to be the hard man. He peels back a chunk of torn seat cover and slips the gun in under the dirty-yellow padding. "Happy now?"

Henry looks at him. "You and me going to have another problem?"

I kill the engine – now the only sound is Jack's wheezy breathing and the rain drumming on the roof. I look in the mirror again and see the State Trooper climb out into the storm. He's on his own – no partner sitting in the car. Maybe we can talk our way out of this after all?

He clumps his way through the rain till he's standing at my window, water dripping from the round brim of his big brown hat.

"Mornin', officer," I say, keeping it light and friendly, "horrible weather, eh?" I give him my best smile.

"Long way from New Jersey," he says in his shitkicker drawl. The guy looks like death warmed up. Bags under his eyes, blue-grey stubble on his chin. Maybe on the way home after a long shift – that's why he's alone.

"Yes, sir."

He sticks out his hand. "Licence and registration."

I tell him it's in the glove box, then lean across nice and slow to open it and pull out the bits of paper. Maybe we're going to get away with it? Maybe he's not going to ask too many questions. Maybe ... He's leaning on the car door, peering in at everyone and I get that fucked feeling again.

What the hell's he going to think? There's me behind the wheel. Henry's in the passenger seat – fifty-eight, V-neck sweater on over a shirt and tie, like a retired door-to-door salesman. In the back we got Jack, with his leather jacket and fucked-up face. And sitting next to him, there's Brian, the eighteen-year-old, pale, shivering blob that used to be Laura's boyfriend, both hands clutching his groin. Thank Christ he's wearing black trousers so no one can see the blood.

The Trooper stares at him. "What happened to your friend?"

"Brian here got himself a dose of something off this girl in Ohio," I say, trying on my smile again and lying through my teeth. "I told him you gotta use a condom, but you know what kids are like these days." My face hurts from all the smiling – let's face it, there's been damn all to smile about these last couple of days, I'm out of practice – but the Trooper seems to be buying it.

"You got a tail light out," he says, then steps back, hooking his finger at me. I open my door and step out into the pouring rain.

It soaks right through my shirt, plastering my hair to my head as I follow him round to the trunk. He points at the offending light.

"Sorry, officer," I say, hoping that this will be it. That he'll get back in his patrol cruiser and fuck off to wherever the hell it is he's going. "I'll take care of it first chance I get."

"Uh-huh." He writes me a ticket, making me stand there in the rain while he copies down the car's registration and my licence details. And then he stops. Frowns. And checks the documents again. Fuck. Fuck. Fuck – he knows they're forged. Fuck! I told Henry we should have used someone more reliable.

5

The Trooper says, "Open the trunk."

"Look, officer, maybe we can –"

He places a hand on the gun at his hip. "Open the trunk."

"Sure thing. Not a problem." Fuck, fuck, FUCK. I slip the key into the lock and twist. The trunk pops open and Mr State Trooper steps up to take a look. Then swears.

I can't blame him, it's not every day you stop someone for a busted tail light and find a dead FBI agent in their trunk. The Trooper's almost got his gun out when Henry smashes him over the back of the head with an empty bourbon bottle.

We stand over the fallen man, watching the blood wash away in the rain.

"He dead?" I ask.

"Will be when I've finished with him ..." Henry pulls out the Trooper's handcuffs, drags the guy's arms round behind his back and snaps the cuffs on. Then we haul him into the trunk alongside Special Agent Mills. It's a tight squeeze – bleeding cop and dead agent – but we make it work.

...

...

And believe it or not: this time we're supposed to be the good guys.

Chapter 2

Ten in the morning and it's still raining like a bastard. We're parked outside a small 7-Eleven clone on the outskirts of Bloomington, waiting for Jack to get back with breakfast, while Henry puts in a call to our boss, Mr Jones. "Yeah," he's saying, the cellphone jammed against his ear, "morgue's still shut ... Uh-huh ... Uh-huh ... We're going round to see him soon as it opens ... Yeah ..."

One of them big minivans pulls up on the other side of the parking lot. Mom, Pop, and two kids. Pop hops out into the rain while Mom stays put to keep an eye on the brats. The guy hurries between the puddles towards the store, stopping when Jack pushes out through the front door. Arms full.

Pop nods a hello, but Jack just gives him one of those shitty looks he's been working on since yesterday lunchtime, when Henry re-arranged his face for him. Pop backs up a couple of steps, then waits for Jack to limp past, before going inside. He looks back over his shoulder at this thug in the leather jacket.

Way to keep a low profile, Jack.

"What?" says Henry, sticking his finger in his other ear, "Oh, right, the kid." He peers over his shoulder at the pale, shivering thing that used to be on the local high school football team. "He's doing OK ... Uh-huh ... Will do. You tell Tammy we're thinking about her ... right." And then he hangs up.

"You didn't tell him about the cop," I say, and Henry shrugs those massive shoulders of his.

"He don't need more stuff to worry about."

Which is true.

The back door clunks open and Jack climbs in. "Breakfast burritos," he says, handing out the little micro-waved parcels. Then it's black coffee for me. Fifth of Old Kentucky, for Henry. And a jumbo Blueberry Squishy for Brian. Jack holds out the bright blue drink and Laura's boyfriend takes it. The kid's hands are shaking, little brown flakes of dried blood falling from his pale skin as he clutches the huge cup of sugar, chemicals and ice. Jack tosses over a small yellow packet. "Advil. They didn't have anything stronger."

Advil, good for a headache, but I get the feeling it's not going to do much for Brian's aches and pains. Poor bastard.

Henry twists the top off his early morning bourbon and takes a swig. That should even him out for a little while. Make him less likely to take another pop at Jack.

I take a bite of my burrito – not bad, but not great. "Mr Jones say anything about the FBI?"

Henry sniffs his breakfast, peeling back the outer layer of the burrito to examine the mess of eggs, ground sausage, potato and cheese inside. "Turns out one of their agents is missing."

"No shit," says Jack with his mouth full.

Henry ignores him. "They're doing an appeal on national TV for Laura tonight. *Fox News* and *America's Most Wanted*."

I nod and take another bite. We always knew Mr Jones would end up on *America's Most Wanted*, never thought it'd be as 'father of victim', though ... "No clues?"

"Nah, you know what these Feds are like, sooner chop off their own dick than tell you anything." He looks back over his shoulder at Brian and his blood-soaked trousers. "No offence." Then downs some more bourbon. "With Feds and cops you got to *persuade* them a little – like with a hammer."

Which is how come Special Agent Mills is now wrapped in plastic sheeting in the trunk of the car ... with a lot of broken bones, his fingernails ripped out, and his face mashed to a bloody pulp.

"You know," I say, finishing off the burrito and starting in on the coffee – which tastes like crap by the way, "we should really get rid of Agent Mills before he starts to smell."

Henry takes a trial bite of his breakfast, chews a couple of times, pulls a disgusted face and spits it out the window into the rain. Then hurls the rest out after it. "How can you eat this *shit?* Jesus ..." Another mouthful of bourbon. "Like someone scraped dog crap off the sidewalk and wrapped it in a fuckin' used condom." He looks over his shoulder at Jack. "What, they don't have no fuckin' donuts? They never heard of Krispy Kreme in fuckin' Illinois?"

"You're welcome," says Jack. "It was that or hot dogs that looked like they been on the grill since Nixon was president. What the fuck you want from me?"

If I was a gambling man – which I am – I'd put money on Jack going back to New Jersey in a body cast. Or a body bag. You see, normal people know not to screw with guys like Henry, but Jack ... I think he's missing that little voice, you know? The one that says, *'Don't poke the fucking bear!'*

"Tell you what," says Jack, "you want something else for breakfast? You go get it. I'm sick of this shit."

Henry carefully screws the top back on his bourbon. Half of it's already gone. I'm hoping that's enough to mellow him out, but I'm not taking any chances.

"Look at the time," I say, starting the car, "we gotta get going. That guy'll be back soon."

Henry's quiet for a moment, then he nods and the top comes off his bottle again. And Jack's escaped another ass-kicking.

* * *

Nearly eleven and we've been sitting in the parking lot opposite the McLean County Morgue for fifteen minutes. It's a crappy-looking building on the corner of West Front and North Main Street, just off highway fifty-one, with a line-up of shitty Fords parked at the kerb. No sign of our guy.

Henry lights up one of his fat old cigars and opens the car window, letting in the sound of the monsoon. I can hear Jack in the back, making pointed 'cough, cough' noises, like that's going to make any difference.

Henry drowns him out by turning on the radio – R&B crackles out of the car speakers and he curses. "God-damn fuckin' jungle music, all drums and shit, these bastards never heard of a melody?" He spins the dial till he finds a station playing Sinatra. "Now *that's* music!" He settles back in his seat, smoking and humming along.

I like Henry, we've been friends for years. But he can be a real asshole sometimes.

Five minutes later a little guy in a white lab coat and Megadeth T-shirt sticks his head out the back door of the McLean County Coroner's office. Big pointy nose, ginger hair, beady little eyes and a goatee beard thing – he looks like a real fucking weasel. He glances up and down the street. Then waves at us.

"Right," says Henry, winding his window back up, "Jack, you stay here with Brian."

"Aw, for fuck's sake, how come I –"

"'Cause I say so. Besides, Brian likes the company, don't you, Brian?"

Laura's ex-boyfriend just shivers. He doesn't say much, not since his meeting with Mr Jones, anyway.

"What if he pisses himself?"

"Then the back seat'll be all nice and warm for you, won't it?" Henry steps out into the downpour. I follow him across the road and up to the morgue where the Weasel is looking nervous, holding the door open for us.

"Hi," he says, ushering us out of the rain and into the stink of floor polish, disinfectant, and whatever it is they use to preserve the dead bodies. The Weasel scurries down the corridor ahead of us, leading the way. "I can only give you fifteen minutes, OK? There's a staff meeting and they'll be back afterwards."

He shows us into the cutting room – all shiny stainless steel and sparkling tiles. There's something on one of the autopsy tables, covered with a white plastic sheet.

"This clears what I owe, right?" says the Weasel. "My little problem with the horses? No one's going to come round and break my thumbs? Right?"

"Yeah, sure, whatever." Henry doesn't really care. "Now show us the body parts."

The Weasel nods, grabs one side of the white sheet and pulls it away like he's performing a magic trick.

And we get to see what we drove all the way out from New Jersey for.

It ain't pretty.

Chapter 3
Laura's Ex-Boyfriend

New Jersey – Wednesday – Two Days Ago

Brian's what you'd call a pain in the ass. Eighteen, on the football team, brown floppy hair, dimpled chin, blue eyes ... exactly the sort of guy a sixteen-year-old blonde girl would fall for. I've seen him at Mr Jones's place a couple of times, picking Laura up in that flashy convertible his mom and dad bought him. No surprise he's a cocky bastard.

Only Brian doesn't look quite so cocky now. He's standing in Mr Jones's living room, trying not to meet anyone's eye. As if we give a shit that he's been crying – we've got more important things to worry about. Like where the fuck is Laura.

"We can only stay a couple of minutes," says Sergeant Maloney, hat in his hands, all respectful like. "FBI's holding a briefing and I gotta be there to make sure everyone's got paper and fuckin' pencils." He stops, looks at Mr Jones's wife. "Pardon my language, ma'am."

I don't think she even notices.

"I tell you," says the Sergeant, "these FBI cocksuckers – pardon my language – are running about like it's *Silence of the* God-Damned *Lambs*. Not one of them ever heard of proper solid police-work."

Henry's standing over by the window, watching as the sweeping headlights of someone's car makes the front yard glow. The FBI have searched the grounds and now they're heading further out. Probably looking for something illegal they can pin on Mr Jones. Bastards. Like he doesn't have enough to worry about with his daughter getting snatched by some sick weirdo.

"I think," says Henry, "Mr Jones would like a word with Laura's boyfriend."

"Right," the Sergeant backs up a pace, "Right, yeah. Of course." He pushes Brian forward.

The kid looks at the carpet, looks at the paintings on the wall, looks at the fireplace, everywhere but at Mr Jones.

"Where the fuck were you?" asks Mr Jones. "Where the *fuck* were you when my little girl was getting taken?" He picks up a glass full of scotch and hurls it into the gas fire.

Brian mumbles something.

"What?" Mr Jones grabs him by the lapels and shakes. "What the fuck did you say?"

"I said it wasn't my fault!" Brian breaks free and smoothes down his jacket. "We had a fight, she didn't want me going to Harvard. She threw Diet Coke all over me. Stormed out of the movie."

"And you didn't go after her?" Mr Jones's voice is low and precise, and all the hairs stand up on the back of my neck. This is not good for Brian. But what does he know? He's eighteen, he's rich, probably thinks he's immortal.

"She said she hated me; was going to take a cab home. I –" He makes a strange squeaking noise as Mr Jones takes a hold of his face and shoves him back, banging his head off the wall.

"You let my daughter, my SIXTEEN-YEAR-OLD daughter wait alone for a fucking cab? In the middle of the fucking night? In the dark? In that part of town?"

Sergeant Maloney can see what's coming. "Come on now, Mr Jones, let's all just calm down. I'm sure –"

Mr Jones smashes a fist into the Sergeant's face and the cop falls to his knees, hands clutched over his nose, blood pouring out between his fingers. Moaning in pain.

"Mark," Mr Jones speaks to me without looking round, "take Sergeant Maloney and get him a drink."

I say, "Yes, sir," and help the guy over to the couch – then hand him a stack of napkins and a large scotch with ice. He dabs his broken nose with one and sips at the other, thanking me.

Brian sees this – sees Mr Jones punch a police officer and the police officer taking it –

and something clicks on in his brain. It's fear. The sudden knowledge that being rich and eighteen isn't going to be enough this time. That Mr Jones doesn't give a flying fuck if Brian's father is chairman of the golf club. That Mr Jones wants his daughter back and he wants her back *now*.

And Brian left her to take a cab home on her own, and some bastard snatched her.

"Henry," says Mr Jones, "go fetch the bolt cutters. I think Brian here's about to have an accident."

It's not a sight I'm going to forget in a hurry.

Chapter 4

Today – Friday – back in the morgue

Henry looks down at what's on the autopsy table, then pulls out his Fifth of Old Kentucky and takes a long swig. He offers me the bottle, and I know I'm driving and everything, but I take a drink anyway. It's not every day you're faced with two sets of severed arms and legs laid out like that.

I don't offer the bottle to the Weasel, just ask him what the hell we're looking at.

"They're arms and legs. Women's arms and legs."

Henry stares at him. "We know they're fuckin' arms and legs. We're not blind!"

I know the Weasel can hear the voice – *'Don't poke the fucking bear!'* – because he hurries over to the counter-top and comes back with a clipboard, flicking through the pages and stammering in his rush to be helpful. "We … we've got another three sets of limbs in the morgue …" pointing at a row of refrigerators "… they were all removed ante-mortem with a sharp knife and some kind of saw –"

I say, "Back the fuck up. Who the hell is Auntie Mortem?"

"Ante-mortem … it means 'before death'. The victims were alive when he cut them up."

"Fuck."

Henry pulls a pair of latex gloves from a box next to the table and snaps them on. Then he leans over and prods at the remains. "Not easy," he says, one hand resting on an upper thigh, "taking a leg off someone who's still alive." He makes like he's got a saw in his other hand, hacking away at the point where the pale yellow-purple skin turns in to raw meat and bone. "They'd struggle like hell.

You'd get blood everywhere." He lets go of the woman's thigh. "Much easier to hack someone up when they're dead."

And he's right. We've done more than our fair share of nasty shit in our time, but we've never cut some poor bastard's arms and legs off while they're still alive. Not to say we've never chopped anyone up, but just, you know, after they're dead.

The Weasel goes pale. "Right ... Yeah ... Er ..." eyes scanning the coroner's report, looking for something that will get us the hell out of his nice quiet morgue, "we're doing a tox screen on the blood, but the labs are swamped right now. They're supposed to be sending an FBI agent down to –"

"Special Agent David Mills."

Weasel nods. "That's –"

"He's not going to make it." That's because he's lying dead in the trunk of our car. But he was nice enough to tell us everything the Feds knew before Henry finished with him.

And the guy goes even paler. "Ah ... right. OK."

"We want details," I tell him, "like: where did they find the bits? How long they been dead?"

"Ah ... that's just it, isn't it? The arms and legs were removed when they were still living. There's nothing to say the victims are dead. I mean with the shock and everything it's likely, but you never know. They could still be alive."

I look at Henry and I know he's thinking the same thing I am. Laura, no arms or legs, trapped in some shitty bastard's basement while he does *stuff* to her. She's only sixteen, for fuck's sake.

Henry growls.

I scrawl my cellphone number on a scrap of paper and tell the Weasel to call me if anything else comes up.

"And you remember," Henry tells him, as we march back through the corridors to the exit, "we never been here. You haven't seen us. 'Cause if I hear that you've been talking, I'm going to come back and make sure *your* arms and fuckin' legs are all they find. Understand?"

Chapter 5

The car's making some strange noises as I pull up and kill the engine. Friday afternoon and we're parked deep in the woods off Highway One Fifty, miles from anywhere. The sort of place you expect to hear fucking banjo music and people telling tourists to squeal like a piggy. The road up here was bumpy, rutted. I bet if it wasn't for the odd logging truck it wouldn't be used at all.

"This OK?" I ask, and Henry nods. He needs somewhere quiet and out of the way to work, where no one's going to hear the screams and call for help.

We climb out into the afternoon. It's stopped raining and the forest floor steams in the sunlight. I go round the back and pop the trunk.

"Jesus ..." Backing away because of the smell. It's not just Special Agent Mills who's rank, the cop stinks as well – I think he's pissed himself. Not surprising.

He stares up at me with terrified eyes. I can see his mouth working on the gag, trying to threaten us, plead, something. Henry and I grab him by the shoulders and pull him out into the sunlight.

The cop tries to get to his feet, but ten hours locked in the trunk with a rotting FBI agent and his legs are like rubber.

"Jack," says Henry, taking off his suit jacket and hanging it on a nearby tree branch, "I need you to get rid of Special Agent Stinky."

"Ah, fuck ..." says Jack, peering out from the back seat, "why me?"

"'Cause I said so." Henry takes off his sweater and it goes on the branch next to his jacket. Then it's the shirt's turn.

Jack swears his way out of the car, "Cock-sucking, God-damned, lousy, mother-fucking ..." He takes a handful of plastic sheeting and hauls the agent's body out of the trunk onto the grass and mud. Jack's feet slither as he drags the wrapped corpse away into the woods. "Got my fucking new shoes on as well ..."

"You know," I say to Henry, pointing at the cop, "we have to ditch the car. They're going to notice this guy's missing – if they haven't already – check what his last call was, and then every cop in Illinois is going to be out looking for us."

Henry stands there in a white undershirt, his US marine 'Semper Fi' tattoo sitting high and proud on his arm. "I think we need to talk about Jack," he says, snapping on another pair of those latex gloves. "What you know about him?"

"He's from the Bronx."

"Yeah, but what's he done?" Henry hauls the State Trooper backwards till the guy's sitting against a tree trunk.

I shrug. "What you mean, what's he done?"

"I mean," says Henry, uncuffing the cop's hands, "you ever work with him before?"

The cop tries to fight back, but his arms don't work. Henry punches him in the face, just in case, then pulls the guy's hands round to the other side of the tree and cuffs them again. He's going nowhere.

"Nope." To be honest, I'd never even met the guy till two days ago.

"So why the hell's he here? You and me, I can see. We've worked for Mr Jones a long time. We got a track record. But Jack ..." He shakes his head and starts unbuttoning the cop's waterproof jacket.

"I heard he came out of Chicago. Did some work for the Palmer family. Strong-arm stuff. Why?"

"I don't trust him." Henry takes out his eight-inch combat knife and runs it along the seams of the Trooper's jacket. Cutting the fabric away. Then he does the same with the guy's shirt, till the Trooper's sitting there naked from the waist up. The cop's crying, the mumbling behind the gag getting even more frantic.

"When a dog gets all mean," says Henry, "they chop his balls off. Like Mr Jones did to Brian there. Maybe we should do the same to Jack."

Henry unbuckles the Trooper's belt, then pulls down the guy's pants, till he's sitting there in nothing but his boots and underwear.

"Jack's just an asshole," I say, "He'll be OK." Besides, I don't want to see another castration for a long, long time. The balls would have been bad enough, but the frank *and* the beans? No wonder Brian doesn't talk much any more.

"Hmmm ..." Henry doesn't sound convinced. He pulls the Trooper's gun out of its holster and twists it back and forth in front of the guy's face. "I think we'll start with this." He sits back on his haunches and places the barrel against the cop's knee. "You're a State Trooper, right? So they'll have told you all about this Sawbones bastard. Like where they found them arms and legs. You're going to tell me all about it. And just so you know I'm not shitting with you, and this isn't all a big hoax, I'm going to blow your kneecap off before we start. OK?"

Behind the gag the Trooper screams.

* * *

"What happened to you?" I ask, when Jack finally staggers back to the car. He's been gone nearly an hour and a half. His jacket and trousers are smeared with mud, his hair's all messed up and his bruised face is twisted into a scowl.

"Fucking fell, didn't I?" he spits. "I fucking hate the great fucking outdoors. What's so fucking, pain-in-the-ass great about it? Fucking trees and fucking mud."

"Well, at least you didn't get eaten by a bear."

Jack freezes. "You're fucking shitting me! Bears? You sent me out there, on my own, and there's *bears*?"

"You got a gun, don't you?"

"Bears ..." He shivers. "And me dragging Agent Bear Snack all over the fucking place."

Henry looks up from what's left of the State Trooper: the poor guy's a mess, but he's still breathing. Just. "You bury him good and deep?"

Jack looks offended. "Course I did. And far out too. Only way anyone's going to find that FBI bastard is with a Ouija board."

"Good. You did good." Henry even smiles. He holds out the Trooper's gun. "You can finish this one off."

No one moves. Then Jack says, "He tell you everything?"

"Oh yeah. They found them arms and legs four days ago, stuffed in a bunch of bins round the back of a diner. Just off the Interstate. Said they think whoever did it was heading East."

"You think he's hiding anything?"

Henry glances down at the Trooper's blood-soaked body. "Nope. He ain't got jack shit to hide anyway. Only lead they got is *maybe* some people saw a dirty Winnebago parked where they found the body parts."

"Then why do we need to kill him? We could just let him go."

There's a pause. "Yeah ... why not? After all we only kidnapped him, stuffed him in the boot with a dead body, tortured him ... I'm pretty sure if we asked him nicely he'd keep his mouth shut."

"I'm just saying, OK? You said he's told us everything so –"

"Hello? Earth to planet fuckin' Jack: he – knows – your – name. He can ID us!" Henry holds the gun out again. "And I *want* you to kill him."

Jack's sweating. "I don't *want* to kill him. You tortured the poor bastard – you kill him."

"See?" says Henry, turning to me, "I told you we can't trust him."

That got a scowl. Jack flexing his muscles. Making himself look bigger. "The fuck you talking about?"

"Me and Mark was just saying," Henry goes over to where his jacket's hanging from the tree and pulls a cigar out of the pocket, "how we don't know you from shit." He sparks up a big silver Zippo lighter and sets the flame to the end. "How you could be anyone."

"I just buried an FBI agent in the fucking woods! With bears!"

Henry puffs, getting the cigar going, then blows out a big cloud of bitter-smelling smoke. "For all we know, you could be a cop."

"A COP?" The bits of Jack's face that aren't bruised purple go bright red. "A fucking cop? You dirty old bastard! You –"

"What did you call me?"

This is getting outta hand fast. "Come on," I say, "this ain't helping."

Henry puts the Trooper's gun on the ground, then turns to smile at Jack. It's not a nice smile. It's the kind of smile you see on a really pissed-off shark before he bites you in half. "I think you and me need to have another chat, sonny."

"I'll do it." It's a little voice, shaky, young. And we all turn to see Brian clinging onto the doorframe of the crappy car we stole in New Jersey. He's trembling, one hand holding on to the place where his equipment used to be. Before Mr Jones took a bolt cutter to it. "I'll kill him."

Henry smiles. "You sure, kid?"

Brian nods, and shambles forwards, each step coming with a wince of pain. "I'll kill him … and you … you take me to a hospital …"

Henry picks up the gun. "How do we know you won't go to the cops?"

"And tell them … what? That … that I shot a State Trooper?"

The kid has a point. Henry hands over the weapon, shows Brian how to cock it – no pun intended – and stands well back. I take my automatic out and hold it loosely at my side. You know – just in case Brian decides to go out in a blaze of glory.

The guy handcuffed to the tree looks up at Brian's pale, bloodless face. The Trooper narrows his one remaining eye and moves what's left of his mouth. We can just hear the word, "Please."

Before Brian blows the guy's head off.

Chapter 6

"You'll find her, won't you?" says Brian as we pull up outside the hospital in Morton, about as far away from where we're going next as possible. He looks a little better since killing that State Trooper. Like he's got a bit of spark left in him.

"Yeah," I say, "we'll find her."

He nods, then sits there, like he's thinking about something. "Mr Jones – will you ask him to send ... you know, my things. Will you ask him to send them here?"

"Brian, I –"

"He said he'd keep them in the freezer – they could stitch them back on ..." He looks at me with those desperate, puppy-dog eyes, wanting me to tell him that some surgeon can sew his dick back on after it's been in the Joneses' freezer for a couple of days. He's not kidding anyone but himself.

"Yeah. I'll ask him."

I pop the door and Brian clambers out, wincing and groaning. He stops, then looks back into the car. "You find the bastard who grabbed her, OK? You find him and then you call me. I want to know that he's dead."

And then he turns and limps through the door marked 'Emergency'.

"You know," says Henry, "never thought he'd do it. Shoot that cop." He smiles. "For a stuck-up college asshole, that kid's got some balls."

We look at each other in silence for a minute, and then piss ourselves laughing.

* * *

"Now this is more like it," says Henry twenty minutes later, settling into the passenger seat. It's the fifth car we've tried in the hospital's long-term car park, and the first he's liked enough to steal.

"Fucking hell," Jack's looking round the back seat, "this thing's ancient!"

"This *thing* is a classic. 1954 Ford Crown Victoria."

It's a huge boat of a car with tailfins and chrome all over the place. Looks like a God-damned juke box, but Henry loves it. "My dad had one of these," he says, running his hand over the dashboard. "He let me borrow it sometimes. Broke his heart when he had to sell it ..."

I check the sun visor – the spare keys are right there. Some people just don't deserve nice things. I crank her up and the V8 engine growls into life, sounding like a smoker on a cold morning.

"Jesus," I say, "think it's going to make it out of the car park?"

"Yeah," Jack leans forward from the back seat, "drive it into the ER. This car needs medical attention!"

"You're a pair of assholes. You know that?"

I shrug and put it into gear. "You remember that when you're pushing this thing down the Interstate, OK?" I test the brakes as we get to the exit. They've got all the bite of a soggy marshmallow. "Where to?"

Henry takes out a notebook – it's got 'ILLINOIS STATE TROOPER' printed in gold on the cover. "According to the cop Brian whacked we got three witnesses ..." I can see his lips move as he skims the page. "One's from Delaware, one's from Chicago, and number three lives back there in Bloomington."

"Shit," I pull out into traffic, "that's two counties away, this thing's never going to make it."

"Just shut up and drive, OK?" Henry pulls his cellphone out and dials directory assistance, looking for a Mr Brian Milligan in Bloomington. He scribbles half a dozen numbers into the State Trooper's pad then starts ringing round. "Yeah, hello?" he says, putting on a fake Illinois accent. "This is Officer Ted Newton, State Police. You the guy who spotted a Winnebago out on the Interstate? Where they found them arms and legs? … Uh-huh … Nah, OK, sorry to bother you." Then he tries the next one on the list.

It goes on for a while – Henry pretending to be some cop making follow-up calls. In the end he gets the right Brian Milligan and they talk for about five minutes, then Henry hangs up and sits there tapping the phone against his teeth.

"He don't remember anything other than it was a brown Winnebago," Henry says at last.

Jack doesn't sound impressed. "Whoop-de-fucking-do. Like that narrows it down. How many brown Winnies out there you think? A million? Two?"

"That's why we're going to pay the guy a visit," says Henry, putting his phone away. "See if we can't jog his memory."

And we all know what that means.

* * *

Ten o'clock and it's nearly dark. We're standing outside Brian Milligan's front door as he peers at the State Trooper ID Henry's holding out. Henry's got his finger over the picture so the guy can't see who it really belongs to.

The guy's old, not ancient – about Henry's age – but his hair's gone south for the winter. There's none on his head, but plenty tufting out the neck of his bath-robe.

"OK," the guy says at last, putting his glasses back in his robe pocket, "you can come in, and so can he, but this one," he points at Jack, "*he* stays out here. I don't like the look of him."

Jack opens his big mouth, but Henry gets in there first, "Most people don't." Then he tells Jack to keep an eye on the car. Which doesn't please Jack very much, but what's he going to do?

Milligan's apartment is a shit hole, littered with empty bottles and cans, two fat blow flies chasing each other around a bare light bulb. The guy wanders over to a tatty armchair and settles back into it, pulling his robe tight around his beer gut. There's a TV in the corner, playing *America's Most Wanted* with the sound turned down.

"I told you on the phone already," says Milligan. "I saw a brown Winnebago. I don't remember nothing else."

A woman comes on the TV screen – talking about some guy who's mailing bits of dead body to various film stars – and I watch her mouthing away as Henry tries to get something useful out of the guy.

"What kinda plate did it have? McLean County? Illinois? Out of state?"

The guy shrugs. "I dunno, do I?"

"Try!"

"I said I dunno, OK? Jesus, you state guys are as bad as the God-damned Feds."

"Well, what colour was it?"

"Brown!"

"Not the Winnebago, the fuckin' number plate, you –"

The woman on the TV vanishes and the next face I see has me scrabbling for the remote, cranking the volume up and shouting, "It's on!"

'... abduction of Laura Jones, missing for nearly three days.' And there she is, on the screen with her name written underneath her picture. Laura Jones: straight-A student, long blonde hair, little round glasses, a smile that shows off a set of braces like tiny railroad tracks across her teeth.

'The FBI are concerned for Laura because of what they found at the scene. We're going live now to Dan Reid.'

And the scene switches to an alleyway, where a man with an umbrella is talking to the camera, 'Thank you, Jane. This looks like any other alley in New Jersey, but this is where police believe Laura Jones was snatched by a serial killer known only as "Sawbones".' A graphic pops up in the bottom left of the screen – a blue high-heeled shoe. 'Police found Laura's left shoe along with what's become this killer's calling card: a hacksaw blade with the words "In God We Trust" scratched into the side. Jane?'

'Thanks, Dan.' And we're back in the studio again. 'As far as police can tell, "Sawbones" has been killing young blonde women for at least three years. Travelling from state to state, he always takes ten victims, then vanishes to lie low for up to a year. The FBI confirms five victims were snatched last week and four more since Sunday, making Laura Jones number nine. Sources within the FBI *believe that if he follows the same pattern as before he's got one more young woman to go.'*

"Typical!" says Milligan, fidgeting with his robe. "You bastards know about this sicko for three years and you *still* ain't caught the son-of-a-bitch." He pokes a finger in Henry's chest. "Round here violating my civil rights when you should be out there catching –"

He lets out a tortured squeal. Henry's got hold of his finger and is twisting it back on itself. Should have known not to poke the fucking bear.

"Aaaaa! Get off!"

"You want to do this the hard way?" says Henry.

"I ain't afraid of you! I was in Vietnam!"

"Yeah?" says Henry, letting go of the guy's finger as Mr Jones comes on the TV. "Which bit?"

"Da Nang, 1969."

Mr Jones doesn't look too good. I haven't noticed before, but he's really starting to look his age. Probably something to do with Laura being snatched. They say it ages people, when something like that happens. *'I wanna say that*

Laura is our little girl.' He blinks back the tears. *'She's a bright, lively, wonderful kid and we just want her back safe and sound.'*

"Da Nang, eh? Who with?"

The old guy sticks out his chest, not knowing that it brings his beer-belly with it. "Magnificent Seventh, Second Batallion."

'Please, if whoever took her is watching this, I know you have the power to give us our daughter back.'

"You was a marine, eh?" Henry smiles. "Semper Fi."

"Damn right, I was a marine! And that's why pieces of shit like you don't scare me."

Which maybe wasn't the brightest thing to say. The smile slips from Henry's face. "Saturday," he says, "10th of February, 1968, four days west-southwest of Hue. Eleven days after the Tet Offensive and you can still see the fuckin' smoke from the burning city, all greasy and black 'cause of the bodies." I've heard this story before. Only once though and Henry was very, very drunk at the time. "We're out looking for one of our recon patrols. No one's heard from them for two weeks.

44

There's six of us slogging our way through the mountains – fuckin' jungle and snakes everywhere. We come across this little village, just some crappy shacks, couple of families. And that's where they were, the recon patrol. The Viet Cong had crucified them on trees all round the village. They'd left the families alive, though. Broke their ankles and wrists, then gouged their eyes out so the last thing they'd see was the patrol they'd given water to being nailed up and gutted."

Henry leans in real close. "It took us three weeks to find the fuckers that did it. And when we did, we made Saddam Hussein look like Santa fuckin' Claus."

The old guy in the bath-robe looks away, then sags back into his chair. On the TV screen Mr Jones is replaced by some scary-looking woman with orange skin and perfect teeth, going on about drain cleaner.

"I don't want to get involved," says the guy, picking at a tomato sauce stain on his robe.

"I don't give a shit what you want." Henry takes his jacket off and unbuttons his shirt. "You're going to tell me everything you know. Starting with that Winnebago ..."

45

Chapter 7

"Where the fuck you two been?" asks Jack when we get back to the car. The wind's getting up again, rain speckling the ancient Ford's windscreen.

Henry smiles. "Had to talk to an old army buddy."

I climb back behind the wheel. "Did you have to dangle the poor bastard off the roof?"

Shrug. "Jogged his memory, didn't it?"

He has a point. I put the car in gear – getting a nasty grinding noise – and pull out onto the road.

"Christ," says Jack from the back seat, "not another one. We're leaving a trail of bodies all over the place … Someone's going to notice!"

"Relax." Henry lights up another one of his stinky cigars. "He's not dead. Just needs to change his underwear. And now we got something the Feds don't." He smiles and opens the passenger window, letting the smoke spiral out into the cold night. "Seems that Winnebago had Iowa plates – Polk County – with some sort of little man on them. And up front, on the dashboard there's a little statue of Jesus and one of them hula Elvises."

He grins, saving the best for last. "And a bumper sticker: 'In God We Trust'."

Yup, it's amazing what being dangled by the ankles sixty feet above a car park can do for a guy with a bad memory who doesn't want to get involved.

Jack leans forward, all excited. "We gotta tell the cops. Call the Feds or something – they can chase down the plate!"

Henry takes a good long draw of his cigar. "Fuck the FBI."

"Oh, come on, you gotta be kidding me! We want Laura back, don't we? They got contacts and shit – computers. They can track him down!"

"And then what? Arrest him? Lock him away somewhere nice and safe where he'll get three square meals a day, Oprah and Doctor Phil on the TV? Pert little nurse with big tits giving him fuckin' sponge baths?" Another lungful of smoke. "Ain't going to happen. You and me both know Laura's already dead. Yeah, she looks like butter wouldn't melt, but I seen her kick the shit out of guys twice her size. Mr Jones taught her all that stuff we learned in basic training – ninety ways to kill a guy with your bare hands. No way some weirdo grabbed her and bundled her off in his shit-brown Winnebago. He'd have to kill her first."

Henry takes the cigar from his mouth and stares at the glowing red tip. "This ain't a search and rescue mission, Jack, this is revenge. We're going to find this Sawbones asshole and we're going to take him back to New York. Where Mr Jones will make sure he spends the last few months of his miserable life in a shit-heap of pain."

I point the car west on the Interstate, coaxing it up to a lumbering fifty miles an hour. Damn engine sounds like it needs the last rites and a decent burial.

It's a shame about Laura – she was a good kid. Smart. Bit kooky, but nice with it. I've known a lot of guys like Mr Jones, and their kids are always assholes. They see their dads with all this power and people afraid of them and shit, and they think they deserve some of that too, just 'cause they're the boss's son or daughter.

Laura was always like a normal person. And she'd make you coffee if her dad was on the phone or something and you had to wait. I liked her.

But Henry's right – if this Sawbones guy has got her, she's dead.

Chapter 8

Laura Jones – Not quite dead yet

It's dark, and it's raining. *Again.* Laura tries to get comfortable, but she can't. The cable-ties dig into her wrists and ankles, not quite tight enough to cut off the blood, but tight enough to hurt. There are more cable-ties looped through her bonds and a set of rings bolted to the Winnebago's floor, making sure she doesn't go anywhere. Her head's pounding. The gag doesn't help much either.

She's sitting with her back to the stove, rocking back and forth as the motor home bounces through yet another pothole. Trying to brace herself so the noose around her neck doesn't choke her as the Bastard driving weaves his way along some God-forsaken back road.

Laura closes her eyes and tries to doze. Maybe if she can get some sleep she wouldn't be too tired to come up with a plan.

A final lurch and the Winebago stops.

One of the other girls – with a bruised face, her eyes like something caught in the headlights of an oncoming truck, starts to cry. Her sobs are muffled by the gag. Not loud enough to drown out the sound of rain hammering on the roof.

There are four of them in here. Laura and three others. None of them much older than nineteen at a guess. All of them scared.

Up front, the Bastard is singing softly to himself – some sort of hymn – and then he pushes through the curtain hanging between the front seats and the living area. *Click* – and a pale, half-hearted light flickers through the back of the Winnebago.

The place is filthy, the carpet covered with dirt and stains that Laura doesn't want to think about. Everything is a mess, the windows covered up with flattened cardboard boxes, held in place with duct tape. It smells of fear and sweat and piss.

Four young women and the Bastard.

He steps nimbly over the crying girl and reaches for the holdall on the table, making sure to steer well clear of Laura's feet. Once kicked in the knee, twice shy. She tries to tell him *exactly* what her dad's going to do to the Bastard when he catches him, but all that escapes the gag is, "Mmmmmgh mmmmmnt, mnnnninmmmmt!"

The Bastard smiles down at her, unzips the holdall and pulls the tazer out, waggling the thing at her. "Now, now. We don't want to be electrocuted again, do we?"

* * *

New Jersey – Wednesday – Two Days Ago

Brian is *such* an asshole. Telling her he's going to Harvard when they're both supposed to be going to Yale. Asshole, asshole, asshole. She storms out of the cinema, throws her head back and shouts it out loud, "Brian James Anderson is an ASSHOLE!"

Harvard.

And he's got the nerve to act all shocked when she pours her Diet Coke over his head.

She wipes a tear away with the heel of her hand. She's not going to cry over him. He's an asshole and a jerk and she wishes she'd never accepted his school pin. They were supposed to be going to Yale!

She stops on the sidewalk and holds up a hand as a yellow cab goes past. Son-of-a-bitch doesn't even slow down. Men!

Of course, what she should do is call her dad, ask him to come pick her up, but then she'll have to tell him why she isn't getting a lift home. And he'll ask her what's wrong. And she'll start to cry. And then Dad will probably get Henry to kick the crap out of her boyfriend. Not that Brian doesn't deserve it ...

Harvard ...

How could he do that to her?

She's not going to cry. She's not ... Yes, she is.

Laura's so miserable she almost doesn't hear it – a pitiful mewing sound. A kitten, in the alleyway. She peers into the dark space between a hair salon and a flower shop, both closed for the night. There's a cardboard box sitting in a doorway, about halfway down the alley, caught in the glow of a security light.

She can see a pair of little fuzzy ears moving around in there.

Laura takes a couple of steps towards it, then freezes, and pulls the pepper spray from her purse. Never hurts to be too careful. But there's no one there, just the cardboard box with a single black and white kitten in it. The poor thing must be hungry. She squats down in front of the box and wipes the tears from her eyes.

"You been abandoned too?" And the tears are there again.

She picks the kitten out of the box, holding the little furry bundle against her chest, turns ... and it all goes into slow motion. A scuffing noise behind her – and she starts to spin round. But she's not fast enough.

It feels like a punch in the kidneys, and then the electricity kicks in, shooting through the muscles of her back, making everything scream. And as her legs give way, and she starts to fall, all she can think of is that if she lands on the kitten the poor thing will be crushed.

Laura's head slams into the alley floor and everything goes black.

* * *

The Back of a Filthy Winnebago – Today – Friday

The Bastard pops the tazer back in his holdall, and picks up the cardboard box from under the table, making cooing noises at the kitten inside. "Who's Daddy's little angel?" he says, "You are. Yes, you are." Then he tucks the box under his arm and walks back through the curtain, singing *The Lord is My Shepherd* as he goes.

The next sound is the driver's door being slammed.

Laura knows that when the Bastard returns he'll have another girl with him. And then they'll be back on the road again. One Step closer to Christ knows what.

Chapter 9

It's nearly midnight and we're driving along the Interstate, listening to some bullshit talk radio station, because that's all this God-damned car will pick up. Henry's sitting in the passenger seat, arguing with the callers – even though they can't hear him – and drinking from a fresh bottle of Old Kentucky.

I can't decide if the smell of bourbon's making me feel hungry or sick.

'*I just wanna say,*' says some cracker on the radio, '*that this isn't about gun control, it's about not treating women with the respect they deserve!*'

"Course it's about gun control, you stupid bitch!" says Henry, "How can it not be about gun control? How stupid are these people? Hello! Wake the fuck up. Isn't about gun control my ass."

"Yeah, well," I say, "what do you expect from people who got nothing better to do on a Friday night than call some lame-ass radio show?"

Jack's in the back, trying to sleep as the counties slowly drift by outside: McLean, Woodford, Tazewell, Peoria, Knox ... We get a small laugh on the way out of Knox – the next county's called 'Henry'. "Hey, look," I say, "you're five miles away!"

Henry toasts the big sign with his name on it as we cross the county line.

Then twenty-five miles later we're driving through the last chunk of Illinois, Rock Island. It's not even eleven miles wide, but it takes us nearly half an hour to cross the border into Iowa. God-damned car steers like a boat, brakes like an oil tanker, and accelerates like ... You know what? I can't think of anything that accelerates this slowly. My fucking *apartment* moves faster than this.

The radio fizzes and crackles as the signal fades, so Henry fiddles with the dial. Back and forth, looking for something to listen to. We almost get a country and western station, but Henry says he'd rather listen to a fat guy farting. And then it's more late night talk radio.

'... *in three weeks,*' says a man's voice. '*OK, you're listening to KFBM – Scott County Radio, all talk, all of the time. We'll be back after these messages ...*' Then it's ads for tractor dealerships and farming shit. '*Right, we're on the air with a regular caller – Jason. What's on your mind, Jason?*'

'*Yeah, you see that* America's Most Wanted *tonight? That Sawbones guy? Travellin' all over the country and snatching girls?*'

'*Uh-huh.*'

'*What I want to know is how come the Feds can't catch this guy?*'

"'Cause they're assholes, *that's* why," says Henry, back into his bourbon again. "Tell you, half the people who call these programmes need locking up. The other half should be taken outside and shot. Back of the head. BAM!"

Then some woman calls in and proves Henry right. *'You know what,'* she says, her voice all nasal, like she's got a cold, or a finger jammed up there, hunting for her brain, *'I saw that Jones guy on the TV going on about his daughter. You know what I heard? I heard he was a mobster. He's out there running drugs and prostitutes and murdering people, and we're supposed to feel sorry for him because his daughter's gone missing?'* She gives one of those sarcastic laughs. *'You know what I call it? I call it God's judgement. "Whatsoever a man soweth, that shall he also reap!" It's in the Bible, people –'*

Henry looks at me, then switches the radio off. He doesn't even bother shouting at it.

"So ..." I say at last, "what we going to do when we get to Polk County?"

Henry shrugs and takes another swig. "We get ourselves a list of all the Winnebagos registered in Polk and we go visit each and every one. When we find the one with a hula Elvis and an 'In God We Trust' bumper sticker, we kick the shit out the owner and take him back to New Jersey."

I nod. Wondering how the hell we're going to get the list, but Henry's a lot smarter than me – he'll figure it out. "You think the Weasel in the morgue was right?" I ask. "That, you know, the girls might still be alive?"

Henry shudders. "Christ, I hope not."

"Yeah ... you're probably right." More miles drift by in silence. "What you think he does to them? You know, after he cuts their arms and legs off?"

"I don't know, Mark," he says to me, "and I don't really want to know."

Chapter 10

The back of a filthy Winnebago

Laura's almost asleep when the side door is flung open. Orange streetlight spills in through the opening, draining the colour out of everything. The Bastard's back and he's not alone – he's got a girl thrown over his shoulder.

He dumps her on the Winnebago's filthy carpet, then climbs in after her, pulls the door shut, and switches on the pale, flickering lights. The Bastard grabs the new girl by the armpits and drags her backwards until she's up against the fridge, then cable-ties her hands and feet to one of the rings bolted into the floor. He's humming *Nearer, My God, to Thee* as he works, with a great big grin on his face.

And then he strokes her leg, starting at the ankle and going all the way up to the fleshy part of her thigh. Squeezing it as he bites his bottom lip.

The Bastard shivers, crosses himself. Then stands.

"Repent," he says, throwing his arms wide, "for the Kingdom of Heaven is at hand." He smiles down at them. "Now we can all go back to the garden."

He ducks back outside, returning with the kitten in its cardboard box, stroking its fur and telling it how good it's been. How special. The Bastard puts the box back under the table, then picks his way between the five women, staying out of Laura's kicking range. He may be a bastard, but he's not stupid.

For a brief moment he sings the opening bars of *Home on the Range*, then he pushes through into the driver's compartment, and switches off the light. The Winnebago's engine rumbles into life.

Laura knows that when they get wherever they're going, it'll make what's happened so far look like a trip to Disneyland. This is just the warm-up act. What comes next is going to be more horrible than any of them can imagine.

Chapter 11

Saturday

Three in the morning and I've got a headache like you wouldn't believe. The car's been getting slower and slower all night, no matter how hard I press the accelerator. Its engine has started making clanking noises, and the effort of keeping the shuddering steering wheel straight is beginning to tell.

Jack's asleep on the back seat with his knees curled up, snoring gently. Henry's dozed off too, the half-bottle of Old Kentucky drained and hurled out the window about a dozen miles ago.

So now it's just me and the rattling cough of the car as something in the engine eats itself. This God-damn thing's going to fall to pieces long before we get to Polk County. And so am I.

I blink at the dashboard, trying to figure out what the little yellow light means. Then I tap the glass and find out as the fuel gauge needle does a rapid crash to empty. Son-of-a-bitch.

Luckily there's a Casey's General Store not far off the Interstate, its red and yellow signs glowing in the pitch-black night. I drive the car down the off-ramp and onto the forecourt.

Henry wakes up as I'm filling the tank. He yawns and stretches, then clambers out into the cold night. "What time is it?" he asks, blinking up at the bright lights – and when I tell him he swears. "How come it's taking so long?"

I grit my teeth. "Because you said we had to steal this ancient, God-damned piece-of-crap Ford Crown Victoria. *That's* why."

He wipes the sleep out of his eyes. "We'll get something faster when we hit Des Moines."

"Sixty, seventy miles. About two and a bit hours in this piece of –"

"OK," he says, "OK, you don't like the car. I *get* it. Fill her up and we'll see if we can't find something a little closer." Henry closes his eyes and shudders. "Gotta take a crap ..." Then he starts towards the store, muttering as he goes, "God-damned morons. Fifty-four Ford Crown Victoria's a classic ..."

I finish filling up, and pay at the pump – using my credit card in the machine – then follow Henry into Casey's. Doesn't matter where you go, pretty much every Casey's General Store is the same. There's a big fat woman, with a basket full of donuts and Diet Coke, arguing with the spotty kid behind the counter about the 'three for two' hot pizza slices.

I ignore her, and go for the hot filter coffee in the far corner. Maybe get some gum too; something to keep me awake for the rest of the drive. And because I'm in a shitty mood, I don't get anything for Jack or Henry.

And then I feel guilty and get a six-pack of root beer and two big bags of tortilla chips. I'm paying for them when I realise there's a

Winnebago on the forecourt. It's brown.
I catch a glimpse of the driver as he sticks the
nozzle back in the pump and pays. A man,
dressed in black, glasses ...

The spotty youth behind the counter tells
me to have a nice day – even though it's half-
three in the God-damned morning. He's
holding out my credit card.

Outside, the guy in black climbs back into
the Winnebago. Fuck.

Probably not him, but I'm gonna have to
check it out.

I'm pushing out through the door when the
Winnebago's engine starts up, its head-lights
sweeping across the forecourt as it turns back
towards the Interstate. That's when I get a
look at the front, there's a little statue of Jesus
and a hoola Elvis on the dashboard. It's him!

Behind me the spotty till-jockey is shouting,
"Sir? You forgot the stuff you bought! Sir?"

"Henry!" I'm running for the car. "HENRY!
GET YOUR ASS OUT THAT DAMN TOILET!"

No sign of him, and I can't wait. I jump in
behind the wheel and crank over that gritty,
crappy engine. It clicks, groans, whines then

grumbles back to life, complaining that I won't let it die in peace.

I tell it to stop fucking moaning and put my foot down. There's a grinding sound as I work up through the gears, swearing to God that this is the last time Henry *ever* gets to pick the car we steal. "Move, you piece of shit!"

"What the fuck?" It's Jack, he's sitting up in the back, bleary-eyed as I throw the Ford round and back onto the Interstate. Following the Winnebago. "Where's Henry?"

"It's HIM!" I say, pointing through the wind-shield at the little red dots in the distance – the motor home's tail lights, "He was getting gas! I saw him, right there on the forecourt!"

"Henry was getting gas?"

"Not Henry, you moron! Sawbones!"

And suddenly Jack's wide awake. "Fuck!" He ducks out of view, but he's back moments later clutching that Glock nine mm of his. Then Jack's left leg appears in the gap between the front seats.

"What the hell are you doing?"

"Getting into the front ..."

We're gaining on the Winnebago. It's slow and it's painful – and the Ford's engine sounds like it's about to explode – but we're closing in.

I slap his foot away. "Will you sit your ass down?"

"God-damnit," says Jack, "Pull over so I can swap seats."

"You have got to be fucking kidding me! Took me long enough to get this piece-of-shit up to forty the first time, I am *not* pulling over."

Something goes CLANGKiGKiGKiG under the hood and I know we've only got one chance at this. I grip the steering wheel even tighter and say a prayer to the God of Dying Automobiles. *Please let this crappy Ford Crown Victoria not fall to bits for ten more minutes.*

"Shoot out the tyres!"

"But I –"

"Just fucking shoot them!"

I check my rear-view mirror to see if Jack's doing what he's told, and that's when I notice the big cloud of grey smoke billowing out the back of our car.

"Oh, Jesus ..." Jack winds down his window and sticks his arm out. There's a hard CRACK and a flash of light as the Glock fires.

Up front I see a little round hole edged in shiny metal appear on the back of the Winnebago. CRACK and there's another one, slightly higher and to the left.

"I said shoot the tyres!"

"You think it's so damn easy, you try it!" CRACK.

The Winnebago starts to pull away from us. The guy driving must have finally worked out someone's shooting the shit out of his motor home. I go to stick my foot down, but it's already flat to the floor. And our Ford Crown Victoria's getting slower.

The engine isn't going CLANGKiGKiGKiG any more, now it sounds like a waste disposal unit eating a brick.

"Shoot the damn tyres!"

Another three shots, all wide of the mark. The Ford's knackered engine makes one last painful grinding noise and gives up the ghost. I can hear bits of crank case pinging loose and bouncing off the bodywork. Steam gushes out of the radiator, all the warning lights come on, all the gauges go dead, and I got no steering.

The car hisses its way to a full stop in the middle of the road. Steam billowing out the front, smoke billowing out the back.

And all Jack and I can do is watch the Winnebago drive away.

FUCK!

Chapter 12

The Back of a filthy Winnebago

The motor home's full of muffled screaming. Laura's trying to push herself as far away from the mess as possible, but the noose round her neck makes it impossible. All she can do is keep her eyes tight shut and try not to be sick. With the gag rammed deep into her mouth she'd probably choke to death.

After a while the screaming settles into sobbing, and then whimpering.

And then something like terrified silence.

It might be an hour later, or it might be two, but at long last the Winnebago leaves the main roads and turns onto gravel. But instead of coming to a halt, it just keeps going, the little stones making a white-noise sound beneath the wheels as they drive and drive and drive ...

They must be miles from anywhere by now.

The Winnebago slows, turns and then lurches from pothole to pothole. Finally it stops.

In the darkness Laura can hear the other girls taking scared breaths. This is it.

The Bastard isn't singing any more, he's swearing as he pushes through from the driver's compartment and turns on the light. The carpet glistens dark red in the washed-out plastic glow, littered with jagged shards of white and clumps of grey.

The muffled screaming starts again.

One of the girls is slumped forward. She's tied up against the motor home's back wall and the top of her head is missing. Blown off by whatever idiot was shooting at them out on the Interstate.

Laura looks away. Tells herself she's not going to be sick.

The Bastard stands there with his mouth open and his eyes like burning coals as he stares at the dead girl. "HOW DARE THEY!"

He storms through the Winnebago, yelling, "SHE WAS MINE!" and when he reaches the girl with no top to her head he kicks her lifeless body. "MINE!" He kicks her again, "MINE!" and again and again, making the whole motor home shake. "MINE! MINE! MINE!"

And in between the yelling and the sound of his foot slamming into the corpse, Laura can hear the other girls screaming behind their gags.

Then the Bastard falls to his knees and cries. Cradling the woman's half-head against his chest, sobbing that he's sorry and they had no right to take her from him.

He sits back and wipes his eyes with a bloody hand, leaving dark scarlet smears across his cheeks. Then he pulls out a pocket knife and cuts through the cable-ties holding the dead girl in place. Drags her out of the Winnebago's side door.

Two minutes later he's back, and someone else is cut free. The girl whimpers as he drags her away. Then the next one. And the next, until there's only Laura left.

He stands looking down at her, his face like sadness carved in stone. "None of your shit, understand?"

Laura nods, the motion stopped midway by the rope around her neck.

The Bastard pulls out his knife again, and holds it against Laura's throat. "Now I gotta go out and get me another girl. You play nice or I can just as easy make it two."

He raises the blade and saws through the noose, then he cuts the cable-ties that go through the rings on the floor. But her wrists and ankles are still bound, the gag's still stuffed in her mouth.

"There we go," he says, putting the knife back in his pocket, "I knew you could be a good girl." The Bastard strokes her hair, smiling. "My good girl. We're going to –"

He doesn't get any further, because Laura head-butts him in the face. SMACK!

By the time he hits the blood-soaked carpet, she's already struggling to her feet – not easy with both ankles cable-tied together.

Weapon. She needs a weapon.

He groans, lying on his side under the table, arms wrapped around his battered head.

WEAPON!

There are drawers on either side of the stove. Hands tied behind her back, Laura fumbles for a drawer handle and yanks the whole thing clean out of the unit. It clatters to the floor – dish towels. Laura swears behind her gag and tries the drawer on the other side. This time it's cutlery, stainless steel glinting dully in the thin light. Forks, spoons, knives that look so blunt they couldn't saw their way through a milkshake, scissors ...

She squats down and feels for them, not wanting to take her eyes off the Bastard. He's still groaning as her fingers find the round handles of the scissors, and fumble them into place. No way she can cut through the plastic holding her wrists together in time. She goes for the cable-ties around her ankles instead, forcing the open blade of the scissors between her skin and the plastic. Then SQUEEZING.

Nothing, nothing, nothing ... and then all at once, snip. She's through.

She stands, eyes darting to the Winnebago's door then back to the Bastard. She can't stab him with her hands tied behind her back, but there is something she *can* do.

Laura takes a big step forwards and kicks him in the stomach. Shouting at him through the gag. Another kick – going for his nuts, but The Bastard curls up in a ball and her bare foot slams into his thigh instead.

If she still had her stilettos on she could stamp on his ugly fucking head till it went right through his skull into his sick fucking brain. But she hasn't, so she hammers her foot into the hands covering his face, hoping to break a finger, or his nose.

And then she turns and runs.

Out through the door and onto the hard-packed dirt of a farm track. The dawn's early light is just enough to make out the shape of a rickety old house. Some barns, knee-high grass, the corpses of long-dead cars.

Laura runs down the road, trying to ignore the jabbing pain of stones as they dig into her feet. Behind her, she can hear the sound of a dog barking. Raising the alarm. She speeds up.

Faster.

The dirt road gives way to gravel and she knows she can't run on that. So she makes for the grass that grows along one side, on the fringes of a field of corn – the stalks taller than she is, rustling in the faint breeze. The grass is cool and damp on her battered feet, but slippery. Dangerous. And running beside the road isn't exactly clever, is it? The Bastard has a Winnebago, and it can go a lot faster than she can.

She has to get off the road. Cut through the field. Find somewhere to hide until daylight. Maybe another farmhouse where she can call for help.

An engine's roar comes from the darkness behind her. He's got over his kicking. Any minute now he'll come racing up behind her and she'll be caught in the head-lights. No place to hide.

Laura dives left, into the corn. Stalks whip past as she runs deeper into the darkness, the leaves slapping wet against her legs and face.

She's making a hell of a lot of noise and she knows it. But not as much as that fucking Winnebago.

Or the dog.

The barking's getting closer.

The Bastard's set the dog on her and it sounds HUGE.

Oh God, oh God, oh God ...

She risks a glance over her shoulder and trips on a clump of something. With her hands tied behind her back she can't even break her fall – Laura slams face-first into the muddy earth between the massive stalks of corn, all the breath leaving her in one painful rush.

She doesn't want to do this any more. She wants to be home in bed. She wants to be safe. She wants to be in the kitchen with Mom, sharing a cup of coffee. She wants to curl up and cry.

But if she does that, he'll catch her for sure.

So she fights her way to her feet and starts running again. The breath hissing in and out through her nose as she pushes herself harder than she ever has before. Running for her life.

The dog's quicker.

She can hear its paws skittering through the mud behind her. Rattling the corn stalks, barking, growling. Getting closer. And closer. And ...

Chapter 13

Des Moines, Iowa

The Fish Trap Lounge is a dingy bar in a concrete strip-mall on Army Post Road. Outside, the sun's baking the sidewalk, but in here it's dark – some people would say the guy who owns the place should get some more lights in here, but they'd be missing the point, wouldn't they? It's *supposed* to be dark. That way no fucker can see what you're up to.

It's half-ten in the morning, and I'm nursing a cup of bitter coffee, trying to blunt the edges with way too much sugar and cream. Still tastes like shit, though. Henry's on Bud Lite with a bourbon chaser, and Jack ... well,

Jack's sulking 'cause Henry tore a strip off him for his lousy shooting last night. Then Jack shouted back how it was all Henry's fault for making us steal that piece-of-shit Ford in the first place. How if we'd stolen a decent car we would have caught the bastard.

So Henry hit him. Again.

The bar's owner is a short, round guy with a shaven head, glasses, a big moustache and a T-shirt with no sleeves showing off a lion's head tattoo. He clatters a big plate of hot wings down on our table and tells us they're compliments of Mr Luciano, whose right-hand man will be here as soon as he's taken care of a little business.

We thank him, and he goes back to whatever the hell it is bar-tenders do when they're not delivering chicken wings and messages for the local mobsters.

Jack picks up a wing and takes a bite, winces, then drops it back on the pile. "Fucking loose tooth ..." He runs a finger around the inside of his mouth.

Henry glares at him. "Don't put it back on the plate! You think we want to eat stuff with your spit on it?"

Thank God, Jack has enough brains to keep his big mouth shut this time as he picks the wing up and dumps it in the ashtray instead.

"I should fucking think so," says Henry, but he doesn't help himself to the pile. Not after spending so long glued to the toilet last night – blaming the breakfast burrito Jack bought him. So that means all the wings are mine. Which is cool.

I'm halfway through them when the front door opens and a big guy in a black and yellow Hawkeyes jacket saunters into the bar and straight over to our table. "One of you guys called Henry?" He's got that strange Iowa accent, the one that goes up and down in the middle of sentences for no reason.

Henry nods at him. The guy looks like he's in his mid forties, getting a bit heavy round the middle, but he carries himself with the same kind of quiet violence you see in grizzly bears. He sits at the table and helps himself to a wing – stripping the meat off the bones as the barman hurries over with a pint of beer and a bottle of hot sauce.

"Right," says the guy when Mr Short-and-Bald goes away again, "I understand you need a favour, Henry."

"For Mr Jones. Yes."

"What d'you need?"

"Winnebago – it's got Polk County plates with a little soldier on them."

"Uh-huh," the guy nods and another wing vanishes. "National Guard plates – it's an infantry man, couple of planes in the background?"

I nod. "I didn't get the registration on account of our car exploding, but it's something like 'Swooner' or 'Stoner'?"

He shakes his head. "Won't be 'Stoner', we got laws against people putting disrespectful shit like that on their licence plates."

"OK," says Henry, "so we're looking for a brown Winnebago that belongs to the National Guard?"

"Nope." The guy takes the top off the hot sauce and splashes it over the remaining chicken wings. "Them there's vanity plates. Don't cost that much. If you're a fire fighter, you can buy fire fighter plates. If you're a war veteran you can buy war veteran plates. For the ones with the little soldier on them, you got to be *in* the National Guard. You got to get your unit commander to certify you're still on active duty every year you got those plates on your vehicle."

Henry leans forwards. "We need an address."

"Not going to be easy. Half the state's in the Guard. Iowa's big on doing its patriotic duty." Another wing gets turned into bones, then the guy downs his beer, belches, and says, "Stay here."

We watch him leave.

Jack scowls at the bar, not meeting anyone's eyes. "I still say we should go to the Feds with this."

That gets him 'the look' from Henry. "No."

"But –"

"I have to tell you *no* again," says Henry, "I'm going to break your arm." He finishes his bourbon and places the glass carefully on the

85

tabletop. "I'm sick of you whining and moaning and not doing what you're fuckin' told. You want to live to see New York again? You keep your fuckin' mouth shut."

Jack looks at him, then at me. For a moment I think he's about to say something, but he doesn't. He does what he's told. Looks like he's finally hearing that little voice. This time he's not going to poke the bear.

Which is just as well. Jack's a big bastard and I don't fancy having to drag his dead body out into the woods to bury it.

Chapter 14

The Middle of Nowhere

Laura comes back to life with a cough, only she's still got the gag in her mouth, so it comes out like a dry retch. Everything hurts – arms, head, chest ... Her left leg stings and throbs ... and it takes her a moment to remember why. To remember where she is and just how fucked up her world has become.

She's sitting in the driving seat of an ancient, long-dead car, both wrists secured to the steering wheel with more cable-ties. She's seat-belted in, but just in case that's not enough, the Bastard has chained her to the seat as well.

The throbbing pain in her left leg is getting worse, and she looks down to see her jeans stained with blood.

It's all coming back to her – the scrabble of the dog behind her, paws on mud getting closer. A sudden moment of silence as it leaps, and then the pain as it sinks its teeth into her leg, whipping its head back and forth, tearing out chunks of meat. The sound of her own muffled screams. And then the Bastard's there, hauling the dog off her, so he can punch and kick her instead. She can barely see out of her right eye now.

Laura tries not to cry. She knows it isn't going to help. But it's no use – she's sore, miles from home, scared, bleeding, and she wants her mom and dad so badly …

She cries till there's nothing left but dry heaving sobs, then even they subside and she's left feeling hollow and empty.

From where she's sitting she can see that the car she's in is one of about a dozen abandoned in a field, all of them axle-deep in the knee-high grass looking like they haven't moved in years. Some have more glass than others, but they're all older models, stained with rust. A graveyard for automobiles.

One of the girls from the Winnebago is chained up in an ancient Volvo. Next to that there's someone else in a Volkswagen Beetle. Another one slumps in a rusty Dodge pickup ... There's an old Ford sitting on flat tyres on the other side – the girl in that one's dead. Her head hangs to the side, eyes open and glassy, flies clustering around the stumps where her arms used to be. Oh, Jesus.

Laura can't twist round very far, not with her hands strapped to the steering wheel, but she can see other cars in the rear-view mirror. At least three of them have dead women in them. There's only one girl still alive back there, chained to the seat of a rusty Cadillac. She's nodding. Back and forth, and back and forth, like she's listening to heavy metal, but Laura gets the feeling there's something broken inside the girl's head. Something that snapped when her arms were cut off.

The girl looks up and stares at Laura. Silently calling for help.

As if Laura can do anything with her torn-up leg and battered body. Like she's not chained to some crappy old car in the middle of a field waiting for the Bastard to come back and hack off her fucking arms! She can feel tears start to prick at the corner of her eyes again, but this time they're tears of frustration and rage as she tries to rip the steering wheel off the dashboard.

* * *

Laura doesn't know how much time has passed, but the sun is still on its long, slow haul up into the clear blue sky when she hears the warning drone of the Bastard's Winnebago. He must have been away somewhere, spreading his own brand of happy fucking sunshine.

A door slams and cheerful whistling fills the air, another bloody hymn. Two minutes later, he turns up in the automobile graveyard, a big shit-eating smile on his face and a girl over his shoulder. Now he has five again.

He stops and beams at them all, chained in their rusty cars. "Rejoice!" he says. "Rejoice for now we are ready to spread the Lord our God's word!" And then he launches into a crackly baritone, singing about how great Jesus is and how he's going to save them all in the end.

But Laura gets the feeling any help from the Lord is going to come too late to do them any damn good. Unless He smites the Bastard down with a big bolt of lightning right now.

The Bastard comes to the end of his uplifting hymn and gives them a salute, before carrying his new girl into a long, low barn that sits at the side of the field. There's no door, just a hole into the darkness inside.

The singing starts again, but this time it's all distorted – echoing inside the barn.

And then there's screaming. High-pitched, terrified screaming.

Chapter 15

The Fish Trap Lounge, Des Moines

It's been nearly an hour and we've still not heard anything from the big guy in the Hawkeyes jacket. Henry's on his third beer with a bourbon chaser. Jack's nursing a grudge and a soda, staring up at a rerun of some baseball game on a crappy little television above the bar. And I'm giving myself an ulcer from drinking *way* too much coffee.

The bar-tender comes round again to see if we want anything, and Henry goes for another beer, even though it's only eleven in the morning.

"Take it easy," I say when the guy's gone away again, "you're going to be shit-faced by lunchtime."

Henry looks at me. "We're not talking about this again."

"I'm just saying, is all."

"Yeah, well, don't." But at least he makes this beer last.

I'm thinking about ordering more hot wings, or maybe a burger, when the guy in the jacket comes back. "This favour," he says, sitting at our table, "it got anything to do with Mr Jones's daughter going missing?"

Henry takes a swig at his bottle of Bud. "You got a name and address for us?"

But Jacket Man ain't put off that easy. "I need to know if this is about that Sawbones guy."

There's silence for a moment, as Henry transfers his attention from the beer to the guy. "You got a name for us, or not?"

Jacket Man stares at him. "I got four brown Winnebagos in Polk County with National Guard plates." He takes a folded bit of paper out of his pocket and places it on the table. "It wasn't easy getting hold of these."

Henry nods. "Favours for favours."

"That's why I gotta know – is this about that Sawbones guy?"

Jesus, he just won't let it rest.

"Yeah," says Henry, picking up the bit of paper, "you and me going to have a problem?"

The guy shakes his head. "You tell Mr Jones this info's compliments of Bill Luciano. Some sick bastard snatches his kid we're going to do everything we can." He nods at the list in Henry's hand. "You want a couple of guys to help?"

Henry stands and slips the note into his inside pocket. "You thank Mr Luciano for the offer, but we got some things we need to do that it's probably best he don't know about, if you know what I mean. Mr Jones won't forget the help."

"Any time." He pulls a business card out of his wallet. "Anything you need, you give me a call."

We say thanks and head out into the sunshine.

* * *

The first address turns up a little old lady with a filthy Winnebago sitting round the back of her crumbling wooden house. She says the motor home belonged to her son, but he got himself shot in Afghanistan, do we want to buy it?

We don't.

Address number two belongs to a couple of junkies, living in a crappy motel with hot and cold running cockroaches. They got a pair of little girls, playing in the car park out front, wearing nothing but filthy underwear. Not even any fucking socks. Henry's all for taking the husband out for a *'drive'*, maybe teach the guy it ain't nice to let your kids go feral like that. But the Winnebago don't got no hula Elvis, little Jesus, or bullet holes in the back, and we're in a hurry, so it's the guy's lucky day.

The third address is for a farm out in the sticks. All the way out the road, Henry's going on about how that asshole back at the motel doesn't deserve to have kids, and how come fuckers like that can get enough cash together to buy drugs but can't afford to get his daughters a pair of fucking socks?

Once we get out of Des Moines, Iowa turns into this huge checker-board of square fields – soy beans, then corn, then soy beans, then corn, then more corn. On and on for miles. It's weird, like someone laid out the whole state with a ruler.

Every now and then we pass a wooden house with a couple of cars in the drive and another out the back, American flag flying in the yard. Mr Luciano's guy wasn't joking about that patriotic stuff.

Jack's sitting in the backseat with the map, muttering to himself every time we pass a junction. "OK," he says at last, "it's the next right."

I take the turning and the tarmac road gives way to gravel. The little stones pinging up into the wheel arches as I follow Jack's directions. About five minutes later the gravel gives out and we're left on a farm track full of potholes.

Jack points at a rambling wooden farmhouse off to the left. "There."

I pull up, blocking in a new-ish looking pick-up. Henry's first out, stretching the kinks out of his back.

"Frank Williams," he says, reading it off the piece of paper Mr Luciano's guy gave us, "he's a chaplain in the National Guard."

"Uh-huh," I pull out my gun, check it's loaded, then rack the slide back and stick the safety on. "In God We Trust."

"Yup."

"Jesus," says Jack, staring at my semi-automatic, "ain't you got a proper gun? Damn thing looks like it came free with a Happy Meal."

"Yeah? Well, maybe I'm not worried about people thinking I got a tiny dick like you." Just because my Heckler and Kotch USP Compact is small, doesn't mean it can't blow a fucking big hole in someone.

Jack grins. "My dick was big enough for your sister. *And* your mom –"

Henry holds up a hand. "Shut it, you two. Trying to do a fuckin' job here ..." He marches up to the farmhouse door and knocks.

Nothing happens.

So we go round the side of the house – there's a chain-link fence making a compound around a kennel, the ground all dug up and speckled with shit, but no sign of the dog that did it. From the size of the mounds of crap, the damn animal's got to be HUGE.

The yard's a mess of trees, long grass and bushes. A pair of blue jeans and a black shirt hang limp and damp on the washing line.

Henry tries the back door – locked. We're talking about kicking it in when Jack wanders off to the other end of the yard, peering back between the trees. Next thing I know he's ducking down and waving at us. Pointing at whatever it is he's found.

It's a brown Winnebago, parked alongside a concrete barn with a sagging tin roof. We can only see the back of the motor home, but that's enough, the rear's peppered with bullet holes and the bumper sticker says 'In God We Trust'.

We've found him.

Everyone checks their guns again.

Jack nods back at the house. "So where the hell is he?"

"I don't know, do I?" says Henry. "Taking the dog for a walk?"

And that's when we hear it – a man's voice singing *Onward Christian Soldiers*, coming from somewhere on the other side of the barn.

Henry gives me the signal and we lope through the long grass to the Winnebago, guns held out at the ready, Jack hurrying along behind. The motor home's side door is open – a quick check shows a sticky red carpet scattered with bits of skull and brain, tie-down rings bolted into the floor and walls, thin bars of light seeping in through the bullet holes.

No one there.

We creep round the side of the barn.

There's about twelve rusty cars abandoned in the long grass, shitty old Fords and Volvos and – "Fucking hell." I tap Henry on the shoulder and point at the Dodge pickup nearest to us. There's a terrified-looking girl chained to the driver's seat, wearing a gag. I take another look at the ancient automobiles and I can see other women, but there's no sign of Laura.

Jack says, "Jesus!" and starts toward the car. He's no more than six paces past the edge of the barn when there's this deep growling sound. Jack freezes, but the growling doesn't stop.

A bloody massive dog slinks out of the long grass, teeth bared as it sizes Jack up.

"Good doggie?" says Jack, even though the fucking thing clearly isn't.

It tenses up, ready to spring and Jack raises his Glock nine mm. "Don't even think about it."

Too late. Suddenly it's bounding through the grass, barking, teeth flashing like knives. And Jack puts a bullet in it. BANG!

The dog doesn't stop. BANG! BANG! BANG! Each one sending a little explosion of red bursting out of the animal's body. The thing's legs go out from underneath it and it slithers to a halt not four feet away from Jack. Damn thing still isn't dead – it lies there whimpering, one paw twitching as it slowly bleeds out.

Jack turns to say something to us, but only gets as far as, "Did you –"

BOOM!

The left side of Jack's face disappears in a spray of blood and bone.

Suddenly everything has gone *very* badly wrong.

Chapter 16

Henry and I hit the ground as Jack's body topples backwards. There's muffled screaming coming from the cars. No one's singing *Onward Christian Soldiers* any more. I give Henry the 'What the fuck just happened?' look and he shrugs, then gives me the signal. I don't need to be told twice, just pick myself up and run round the back of the barn, keeping low – past the Winnebago with its blood-soaked carpet – coming out on the other side.

I can see Henry creeping towards the barn's entrance, so I do the same. Him going in from one side, me from the other: your classic pincer movement.

Henry peers round the edge of the opening then yanks his head back as another shotgun blast rips through the air, sending chips of concrete flying. He holds a finger up to me. One – there's only one of them.

I nod and drop to my belly, crawling along through the grass until I'm level with the entrance, keeping as quiet as I can as Henry shouts, "We've got the place surrounded! Get your ass out here, or we'll come in there and blow it off."

BOOM! More concrete explodes. At least he's shooting at Henry's side of the doorway, not mine. By now I'm close enough to see into the barn's crumbling interior. There's farming crap stacked against the walls, a couple of bales of straw and some weed-killer in the corner. But what catches my eye is the old wooden table in the middle of the barn. Someone's chained to it. I can see their hands and feet hanging over the edges. There's no sign of the son-of-a-bitch who killed Jack.

Blood drips off the lip of the table – slow, dark and sticky. Not fresh, but not old enough to congeal.

Holy shit ... There's a big plastic bin-bag under the table with a couple of arms and legs poking out of it.

And then whoever it is on the table groans.

I glance at Henry and he tries the 'come out, we've got you surrounded' thing again. This time when the son-of-a-bitch shoots I'm ready for him. He's got his back to me as he brings this huge shotgun up to his shoulder and pulls the trigger. And in the silence following the deafening BOOM! I put a bullet in the guy's knee.

It goes in as a tiny hole, but when it rips out the other side it takes his kneecap with it – blood and bone bursting over the table legs.

He screams and falls. The shotgun clatters against the barn's concrete floor, where it goes off again. BOOM! Buckshot whistles over my head as I bury my face in the grass.

I look up for long enough to shout, "He's down!" then I'm on my feet, hurrying into the dark barn, my gun trained on the son-of-a-bitch's head. Not that he's any threat to us now, he's too busy clutching the place where his knee used to be and screaming.

Henry says something, but I can't hear him, I'm looking down at the woman chained to the wooden table. It's Laura – stripped down to her underwear, rubber tubing tied around her upper arms and thighs, cutting off the blood before he cuts off the limbs. She's covered in bruises, her face all puffy and swollen.

She looks at me with one wide, angry eye, her mouth working behind the gag, but all that comes out is this furious mumbling. I hurry over and undo the filthy rag he's tied around her mouth.

"Agh! Jesus!" She turns her head and spits. "Fucking bastard!" I get to work on the chains holding her to the table while she swears. "What took you so long?"

"Are you OK?"

"Do I look fucking OK?" Laura tries to move, but nothing works – her limbs are slowly turning purple. "Bastard ..." Then she asks me, "Is he alive?"

I look down at the man – he's gone all quiet, rocking back and forth, still holding his ruined knee. "Yeah," I say, "he's still alive."

Then I start untying the rubber tubing from her arms and legs.

She grits her teeth as the blood starts to flow again. That's got to be one of the shittiest doses of pins and needles ever.

After a couple of minutes Laura swings her legs over the edge of the bloody table then drops to the floor, her legs give way and I have to catch her. There's a chunk missing from her left leg, surrounded by teeth marks. She hisses in pain, holding onto the edge of the table to stay upright.

She's shivering, so I offer her my jacket. Laura smiles as she puts it on, but it's not a nice kind of smile.

"Henry, Mark," she says, "get the Bastard on the table. And chain the fucker down."

I shake my head. "Can't do that, Laura, your dad wants him alive."

She stares at me, and suddenly she don't look like Laura no more – she looks like her old man when he tells Henry and me someone's stepped outta line and we gotta go whack them ... "He say he had to be in one piece?"

"Laura –"

"Look at that leg, Henry. We don't get him some medical attention soon, he's going to bleed to death."

"But –"

"Best thing for him," she says, picking a big knife off the tabletop, "is ampu-fucking-tation."

Chapter 17

We manage to talk her down to just the one leg. And when the screaming's stopped and the guy's passed out, we drag him and his amputated limb out to the car and bundle him in the trunk. He looks like shit, but he'll survive the trip back to New Jersey. I ain't saying how long he'll live after that though. Let's just say I wouldn't want to be in his shoe when we get there.

I make sure Laura's comfortable in the passenger seat, then go join Henry in the graveyard of dead cars.

"How long before we're back home?" he says.

I shrug. "Thousand miles ... what's that, about seventeen hours? I could do it in fourteen, but no way in hell I want some cop pulling us over for speeding with Long John Fucking Silver in the boot. Should be back in New Jersey about six tomorrow morning."

Henry nods, then looks out at the cars and their terrified inhabitants. The one nearest to us is in an ancient Cadillac – she's rocking back and forwards in her chains, the stumps where her arms and legs used to be moving in little circles, crawling with flies. Her eyes are tight closed and I swear to God if I'd known what Henry was about to do I'd have stopped him.

But I don't know.

Not until he pulls his gun and puts a single bullet through her head.

BANG!

"Fucking hell, Henry! What you do that for?"

He watches as her torso twitches then hangs still against the chains. "Rule number one, never leave witnesses." He bends down, picks up the brass casing from his bullet and puts it in his pocket – that's rule number two, never leave any evidence. We've already picked up all our brass from outside the concrete barn. "Besides," he says, "what kinda life she going to have, no arms and no fuckin' legs?"

He turns his gun on the next one, chained to the seat of a rusty Volvo.

"Henry!"

"What?"

I bring my gun up and point it at Henry's chest. "No."

He stares at me for a second, then goes back to the girl in the Volvo. "I don't make the rules."

"Henry, look at her – she's sixteen, for fuck's sake. She's scared, she's done nothing wrong."

"Never point a gun at someone you're not prepared to kill."

He points the gun at her head and the girl closes her eyes, sobbing behind her gag.

"Don't fucking do this!"

"God," he says, "you're just like Jack –"

And that's when I shoot him.

Chapter 18

We're already halfway across Illinois when the news comes on the radio – *'Following an anonymous tip-off, police raided a farm on the outskirts of Polk County, Iowa this afternoon and discovered what's being described as something out of a horror film. Sheriff Oswald and his team found the bodies of five dead women chained inside abandoned automobiles on the farm of plumber Frank Williams.'*

I turn the volume down a bit, because Laura's finally fallen asleep and I don't want to wake her. She's got a cardboard box in her lap, and every now and then I can hear that kitten shifting about in there, mewing.

'Williams – a chaplain in the National Guard,' says the news reader, 'is missing, but police now believe him to be the serial killer "Sawbones". A nation-wide manhunt is now underway.'

Not that they're ever going to find him. By the time Mr Jones has finished with the son-of-a-bitch there won't be enough left to fill a lunchbox.

'Three young women, abducted earlier in the week, were discovered in Williams' home, suffering from trauma and shock.'

Which only leaves ...

'A fourth woman was dropped outside Mercy Medical Centre in Des Moines. Hospital sources say surgeons are battling to re-attach her arms and legs, but the outlook is bleak ...'

I listen for a bit longer, making sure they don't say anything about Jack and Henry – then I switch over to something a bit more cheerful. I'm going to miss Henry, but it's nice not to have to put up with his shitty taste in music.

As I flick through the stations I hope that Mr Luciano's men got Henry to a doctor in time. He was bleeding pretty badly when

Laura and I left. The guy in the Hawkeyes jacket said, 'Anything you need, you give me a call.' So I asked for a good doctor who don't ask too many questions, like, 'Who the fuck shot you in the back?' If the old bastard doesn't die on the operating table he's going to be fucking pissed when he gets out.

And I hope they buried Jack somewhere nice, not just fed him to the pigs. Yeah, he was an asshole, but ... well, you know. You look after your own.

Two hundred miles later I'm humming along to some old Elvis Presley number, sticking to the speed limit, when I see the red, white and blue flashing lights in my rear-view mirror.

Fuck.

Laura yawns and sits up in the passenger seat, her face a confusion of fuzzy sleep and not knowing where the hell she is. For a moment it's like she's still a sixteen-year-old girl, a nice kid who loves her parents and respects her elders. Then she remembers what's she's been through since she was snatched from that alleyway in New Jersey and her face goes hard. Like it was when she took that guy's leg off.

She reaches into the box with the kitten in it and comes out with Jack's Glock nine mm.

And that's when I know we're fucked ...